The Farmer's Wife

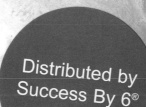

by Idries Shah

Illustrated by Rose Mary Santiago

ONCE UPON A TIME there was a farmer's wife.

One day when she was picking apples from a tree, one of the apples fell into a hole in the ground and she couldn't get it out.

She looked all around for someone to help her, and she saw a bird sitting on a nearby tree, and she said to the bird, "Bird, Bird, fly down the hole and bring back the apple for me!"

But the bird answered, "Tweet, tweet, tweet," which means "No."

He was rather a naughty bird, you see.

And the farmer's wife said, "What a naughty bird!"

And then she saw a cat, so she said to the cat, "Cat, Cat, jump at the bird until he flies down the hole and brings back the apple for me."

But the cat said, "Miaow, miaow," which means "No."

She was rather a naughty cat, you see.

So the farmer's wife said, "What a naughty cat!"

And then she saw a dog, so she said to the dog, "Dog, Dog, chase the cat until she jumps at the bird, until he flies down the hole and brings back the apple for me."

But the dog said, "Bow-wow-wow," which means "No." He was rather a naughty little dog, you see.

So the farmer's wife said, "Good gracious, what a naughty little dog!"

Then she looked around and she saw a bee and she said, "Bee, Bee, sting the dog until he chases the cat, until she jumps at the bird, until he flies down the hole and brings back the apple for me."

But the bee said, "Bzz-bzz," which means "No." He was rather a naughty bee, you see.

So the farmer's wife said, "Good gracious! What a naughty bee!"

Then she looked around and she saw a beekeeper, and she said to the beekeeper, "Beekeeper, Beekeeper, tell the bee to sting the dog, until he chases the cat, until she jumps at the bird, until he flies down the hole and brings back the apple for me."

And the beekeeper
said, "No, I won't."

So, the farmer's wife
said, "Good gracious!
What a naughty
beekeeper!"

And she looked around again. This time she saw a rope on the ground.

And she said, "Rope, Rope, tie up the beekeeper until he tells the bee to sting the dog, to chase the cat, to jump at the bird, to fly down the hole and bring back the apple for me."

But the rope didn't take any notice at all. It just lay there. And the farmer's wife said, "Good gracious! What a naughty rope!"

And then she looked around and she saw a fire.

And she said, "Fire, Fire, burn the rope until it ties up the beekeeper, until the beekeeper tells the bee to sting the dog, to chase the cat, to jump at the bird, to fly down the hole and bring back the apple for me."

But the fire said nothing at all. It just didn't take any notice. It wasn't going to burn the rope.

"Good gracious!" said the farmer's wife. "What a naughty fire!"

And she looked around again and she
saw a puddle of water.

And she said, "Water, Water, put out the fire,
because it won't burn the rope, because it won't tie
up the beekeeper, because the beekeeper won't tell
the bee to sting the dog, because the dog won't
chase the cat, because the cat won't jump at the
bird. And because the bird won't fly down the hole
and bring back the apple for me."

But the water didn't take any notice at all. And
the farmer's wife said, "Good gracious! What
a very naughty puddle of water you are!"

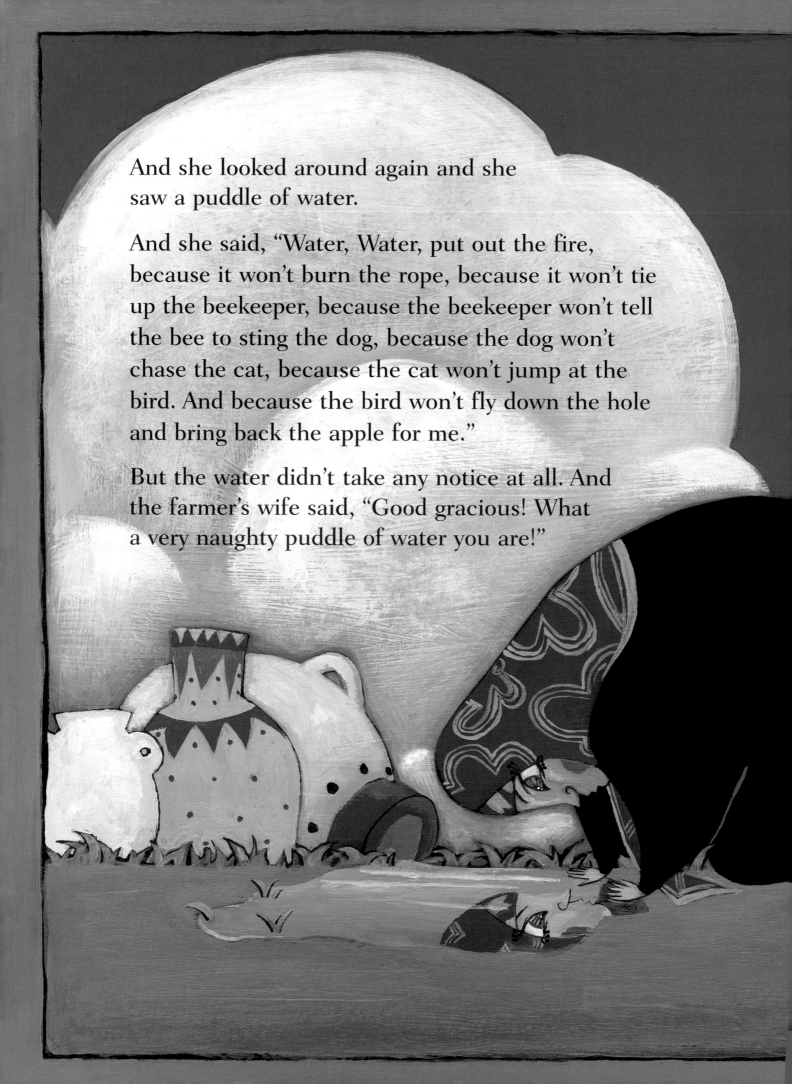

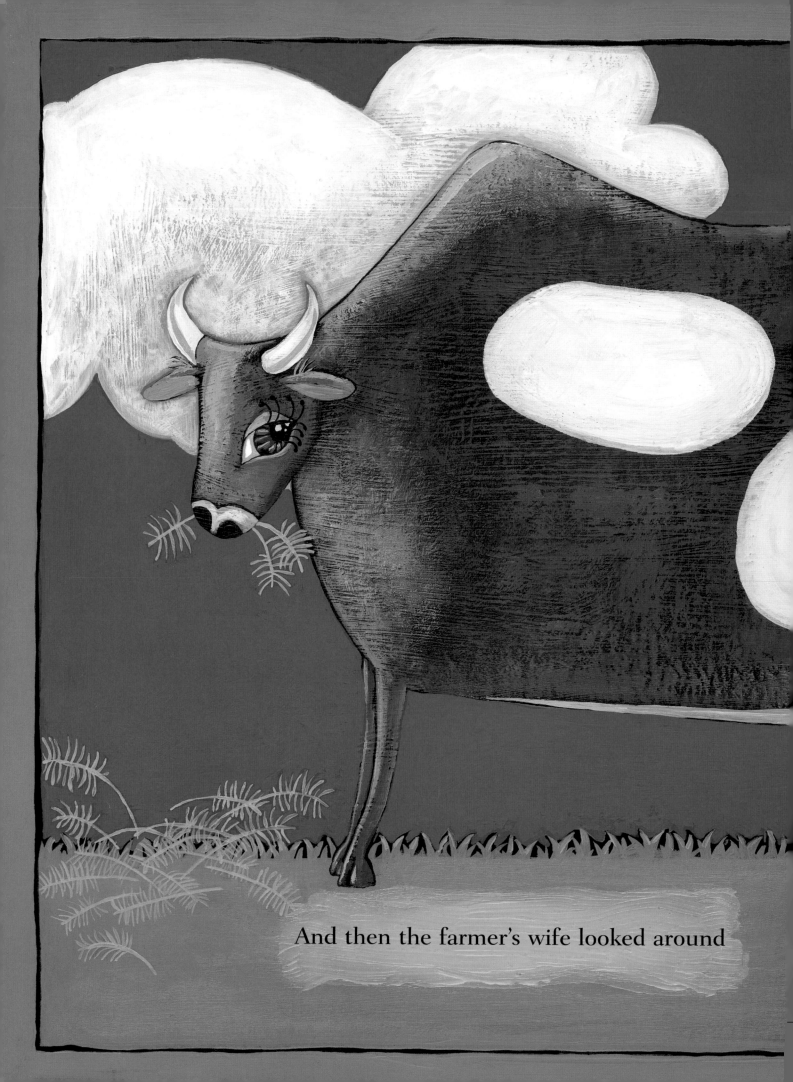

And then the farmer's wife looked around

and she saw a cow.

And she said to the cow, "Cow, Cow, drink up the water, because it won't put out the fire, because the fire won't burn the rope, because the rope won't tie up the beekeeper, because the beekeeper won't tell the bee to sting the dog, to chase the cat, to jump at the bird, to fly down the hole and bring back the apple for me."

But the cow only said, "Moo, moo," which means "No." And the farmer's wife said, "What a naughty cow!"

And then the farmer's wife looked around once more and she saw the bird again.

So she said to the bird, "I want you just to peck that cow a little."

So the bird said, "All right, I don't mind pecking that cow. As long as you don't expect me to fly down the hole and bring back the apple for you."

The farmer's wife said, "You just peck the cow."
So, the bird, who was a bit naughty, pecked the cow.

And the cow started to drink up the water,
and the water started to put out the fire,

and the fire started to burn the rope, and
the rope started to tie up the beekeeper,

and the beekeeper started to tell the bee, and the bee started to sting the dog, and the dog started to chase the cat, and the cat started to jump at that very same bird that had pecked the cow.

And then the wind flew down the hole and

brought back the apple for the farmer's wife.

And everyone lived happily ever after.